LAKE SHORE BAPTIST CHURCH
P.O. BOX 670
LAKE DALLAS, TX 75065

In Memory of
Holly Pearson

Lake Shore Baptist Church

NINGIYUK'S IGLOO WORLD

NINGIYUK'S
IGLOO WORLD

by

Anna E. Rokeby-Thomas

Pictures by

James N. Howard

Lake Shore Baptist Church

MOODY PRESS
CHICAGO

Second Printing, 1973

ISBN: 0-8024-5935-8

Printed in the United States of America

To my granddaughters —

Heather Ann McLean
Megan Anne Rokeby-Thomas
Jennifer Ann McLean

Contents

1

The Awful Secret

Ningiyuk's world of ice and snow has many names. In the summer it is called the Land of the Midnight Sun. But in the dark winter months it becomes the Land of the Midday Moon. The few white people who were huddled in the tiny settlement called it an Arctic island.

"And it's far north of central Canada!" the missionary's wife told her large group of Eskimo children after Bible story time.

"But what is Canada?" Every native wanted to know. The outside world was very strange to them.

Usually ten-year-old Ningiyuk was a happy child. But today she kept wishing that she were an Eskimo boy instead of a girl. Without even listening she could hear her brother, Okio, playing in the sunshine with their husky pups. "But I'm shut up in this dingy igloo," she muttered crossly. "And here I'll have to stay until I can make fine stitches in this tough old hide."

"By the time I had seen the sun return ten times, I could sew like a grownup," Grandmother Itow reminded her sharply.

Ningiyuk gripped the caribou skin on her lap and impatiently jerked the sinew-threaded needle through the mean leather. "Ouch!" The curved needle had pierced her finger. "Surely it would be easier to hunt bears than to get wounded like this." She waved her arm back and forth in motions of distress.

"But you don't listen to what I tell you. And see, you're not holding the skin the right way." With endless patience the old lady began teaching her all over again.

"I know, I know," Ningiyuk admitted. "But how can anyone be expected to sew with bleeding fingers?" She began licking her raw fingertips with her tongue.

"You'd better watch me for a while." Itow took the sewing from the child's lap.

Ningiyuk sighed with relief. Quickly she pillowed her back with furs and squirmed into a comfortable position against the snow wall. *This might even be fun,* she thought.

But watching the old lady's gnarled fingers at work soon became tiresome. Grandmother's face was much more interesting! Many long years ago she had proudly endured being branded with tattoo markings in true tribal fashion. It had taken hours of patient suffering. But without flinching she had sat while the perforated lines were filled with fine, blue soapstone powder which had been mixed with some soot from the blubber lamp. Today the weird purple lines that streaked away from her mouth seemed to come alive! Itow's brown leathery face was kept in motion all the while she weaved the curved needle in and out through the caribou skin. The purple lines danced back and forth in perfect rhythm. Sometimes they almost reached her ears.

I wonder if I'll be ugly when I grow old? Ningiyuk thought, as she looked with pity at the old lady's wispy dull hair. Worse than that, Itow's faded eyes were haunted with fears. The evil spirits gave her no peace.

"Did you ever have teeth?" Ningiyuk asked, kindly.

"I had teeth as white and even as your own." Itow looked up in surprise. "And I still have my teeth! The difference is they are worn even with my gums and are hard to see." A faint smile crossed her tired face as she added, "But I can match anyone when it comes to chewing the soles of seal boots. These worn-down teeth serve me well."

"I'll not wear my teeth away on anybody's boots!"

"Such talk for an Eskimo girl!" Itow pointed to the snow tunnel. "You'd better go outside and play. The winter will be long."

Ningiyuk jumped to her feet. In seconds she was bundled in furs and dashing for the door. Then she turned and went back. With love in her eyes she laid her soft young cheek against the brown wrinkled face and they rubbed noses. There was deep affection between them.

Outside, the world looked golden, for the sun was still in the sky. Ningiyuk ran over the drifts as fast as her short legs would carry her. When she reached the top of the hill, she gasped at the beauty of the setting sun. Then she closed her black, slanted eyes and pretended the sun had vanished. "Surprise!" she exclaimed, opening her eyes wide. Then she laughed at her own foolishness.

"You're talking to the sun again!" Okio startled his sister from behind. "Sun worship is evil. I'm going to tell on you."

"It isn't sun worship," Ningiyuk stamped her foot down angrily. "The sun sends out happiness and can be your friend. You ask our grandmother. She knows everything."

"Indeed she doesn't." Okio suddenly looked sad. "Our grandmother refuses to listen to the good words of the missionary. But our father listens," Okio spoke reverently, "and now he is not only a mighty hunter. He is a **mighty man!**"

"Our grandmother is too old to understand the message." Ningiyuk defended the old lady. "And just why did you come here to quarrel with me? Surely you know that I like to watch the sunset in peace."

"You are wrong," Okio answered with a wise expression. "Father Komoyiok says the message of the missionary is simple enough for a child to understand." Then he shrugged his shoulders as though to leave. "And I came here to tell you a secret. It's all about *you*. But I can keep it."

"Tell it to me. Please!" Ningiyuk faced him. Her eyes sparkled with happy excitement.

Okio loved to tease his sister, and this was the best chance he had had for a long time. But finally she persuaded him to talk. "Last night after you were asleep, I heard our parents whispering. I guess they thought I was asleep, but I heard every word they said." Okio rubbed his brow as though he wasn't quite sure how to make the most of his big secret. "They said that in another year they'd better tell you who you really are. It seems you belong to a tribe of Eskimo to the west of us. So—that means you really aren't my sister. You don't even belong to our tribe. How does it feel to be—?"

"It's a lie!" Ningiyuk cried out as though her brother had struck her. Fiercely, she grasped his arm and shook him. "Stop teasing me! Tell me your secret. The truth, I mean."

"I told you what I heard, nothing more and nothing less." But Okio's grin was gone. He felt strangely uncomfortable.

"It's a lie!" Ningiyuk kept repeating. But down in her

aching heart she knew it could be the truth. Both knees went limp as she slumped down on the snowdrift. "I belong to another tribe. And I'm—I'm adopted." She spoke scarcely above a whisper.

"That's nothing to be sad about. Lot's of people are adopted." Okio wished he had kept his secret to himself. "There's no need to act like a fox caught in a trap." He felt confused now that her suffering reached out to him. With many kind words he tried to comfort her.

But Ningiyuk didn't hear a word that he was saying. She didn't even notice when he finally left her alone. What she did know was that the beautiful white world she gaily had raced into had suddenly changed. It looked black and horrid now, and seemed to be crumbling all around her. Her friend, the sun, had dropped out of sight, and a frightening black cloud filled the sky. *I must be dreaming.* Her teeth chattered as she stared into space.

"It's long past the time you should be in your igloo." Her father's voice brought her to her feet.

Ningiyuk looked up at Komoyiok as though he were a stranger. Then she broke down and sobbed as though her heart were breaking. The mighty hunter was shocked when he heard her say, "You're not my father, not my *real* father."

2

An Igloo Dream

Komoyiok's stern face turned red. As a hunter his life had been too busy to spend much time with the little girl in his igloo. Now he felt awkward. But a strange tenderness came over him as he looked down at her. The round fat face that looked up at him had always worn a smile and there was a dimple in her chin. Not many children had skin so tawny and healthy. It glowed like the copper knife he held in his hand. When she raced with the wind, he thought of a caribou fawn, for her toes scarcely touched the rocks. Ningiyuk was swift and graceful.

The strong man knelt down and looked with pity into her troubled eyes. "It is true you are not our own child. You were given to us when only a few days old. I speak no soft words of love, for that is not my way. We have tried—" Komoyiok stopped in the middle of the sentence and stared far into space. Words were difficult for him. "Ten times the sun has disappeared and returned since we brought you to our igloo. Has your mother not cared for you well? And have you ever gone hungry for long periods? What more can an Eskimo girl want?"

"Nothing, except—I mean, nothing," Ningiyuk managed to say.

As Komoyiok stood up, he pulled her close to his side and went on explaining. "Surely you know it is the custom of our people to give their babies away if they wish. There are many reasons why they do it. Almost as soon as it is done the family forgets the child is not their own. Often old people adopt a baby to cheer them in their last years. Be glad that you were taken into a family and not treated like a plaything." He patted her on the head.

Slowly, they walked toward the igloo. He held her hand in his. Never had Ningiyuk felt so much affection from her father, and his kindness brought some warmth to her cold, shivering body. It gave her the courage to ask the question that was spinning in her mind. She could think of nothing else. "But why didn't my parents want to keep me for themselves?" she asked.

Komoyiok stopped in his tracks. He grasped her shoulders and shook her harshly. "All girls ask that question. Then they start thinking about their other home and cry to get there. Why else have we kept this news from you?" His voice was severe. "There will be no more talk about your being adopted until I speak of it myself."

When they entered their igloo, a hushed silence came over everyone inside the white dome. Okio was holding his head low because Mother Atuk had scolded him sharply. "A hot meal is a cure for everything," the lady of the igloo said, as she stirred the stew in the large pot that hung over the seal oil lamp. Father Komoyiok remembered to thank the Great Spirit before the family started to eat. But Ningiyuk's appetite was gone, and she didn't touch one bite of the food.

"Go to your sleeping bag," her mother ordered.

For once Ningiyuk was glad to go to bed. Quickly, she pulled off her fur garments and crawled into the friendly fur bag. But the snow wall she faced wasn't friendly. To-

night she could see no fairies dancing as the light flickered on the frosty surface. They had become frightened animals in a storm. She closed her eyes, but sleep wouldn't come. There was that spinning feeling in her head that kept sending pains all the way down to her heart. *I'll pretend I'm asleep.* Ningiyuk closed her eyes ever so tightly.

Then her thoughts began to drift away beyond the igloo. Far in the distance she could hear voices, and people began to appear. They were very dim at first, but the picture became clear. *It must be a celebration,* Ningiyuk thought. *Everyone seems so gay and happy.* They waved a friendly welcome and Ningiyuk walked toward them. She felt drawn to one person, a lady dressed in white furs.

"I know you! I know you!" Ningiyuk forgot her shyness and began to run. Suddenly, she stopped in her tracks. The lady was *so* beautiful that Ningiyuk felt spellbound. "I'm looking at the most beautiful person in the whole world," she gasped.

At first the lovely lady didn't notice her. There was sadness in her kind eyes, as she watched the children at play. She seemed to be searching for someone. Then she saw Ningiyuk. "My own little girl! I've found you at last!"

Ningiyuk threw out her arms to hug the lady. They struck the snow wall! It was all a dream, a lovely igloo dream.

As though to hold the dream inside the sleeping bag, Ningiyuk pulled the top flap of fur over her head. *That must have been my mother, my real mother,* her mind was filled with flashing thoughts. *I'll keep her picture inside my heart, and someday I'll find her,* she vowed to herself. Somehow she felt a lot better and was soon in a dreamless sleep.

All the next day Ningiyuk stayed inside the igloo. She was quiet and pale. No one felt gay or talkative. Finally Atuk tried to persuade her to go outside and play.

"Please! I'll sew until my fingers are raw. I'll scrape skins and do igloo chores. But I can't bear to have the children stare at me with their sorry eyes."

"I've no patience with such foolish talk." Mother Atuk frowned. "Many of the children that you play with are adopted. Some of them are shuffled back and forth so much that they don't know where they belong."

"But they're used to being adopted!" Ningiyuk looked up imploringly. "I got used to being the daughter of the mighty hunter. Always I was happy. And there was envy in the eyes of the other girls because of my fat cheeks and many fur outfits. Now it's all so different." Tears trickled down her cheeks.

"You are still the daughter of the mighty hunter," Atuk told her impatiently. And with some pride in her voice she added, "And you still will wear the finest clothes."

"Whose child am I?" Ningiyuk asked impetuously. "To what tribe do I belong?" A sudden desire came over her to tell Atuk about the dream. She felt she must know if the lovely lady was her real mother.

"Your father has spoken! His word is law in our igloo. You are to stop asking foolish questions."

Ningiyuk shrank back against the snow wall at the harsh sound in Atuk's voice. She hid the beautiful dream deeper in her heart. It would have to be her very own secret. But the thought of the dream brought back a spark of happiness. "Are the Eskimo tribes to the west of us much different from our tribe?"

"Indeed, they are different. Most of them speak the white

man's language and live in wooden houses. I fear they have forgotten how an igloo is built and have grown soft."

Ningiyuk looked toward the west and became excited. She could picture her lovely mother living in a white man's house. "It must be nice to live their kind of life. Perhaps —" She stopped abruptly. The expression on Atuk's face was like a storm cloud.

There never had been much affection between Ningiyuk and the tall angular woman, whom she thought was her mother. Atuk was strong and brave. She could sew fine stitches and seemed willing to work her fingers to the bone without complaint. *But she forgets to look at the beautiful things, like the sun, so her face stays solemn,* Ningiyuk thought sadly. *Even when her work is done at night, she never plays games or sees pictures in the spluttering seal oil flames. Instead, she sits staring into space, as silent as a soapstone carving.* A look of despair came over Ningiyuk as she thought of the barrier between them.

Grandmother Itow seemed to be reading her thoughts. She reached out and touched the child's arm. "How would you like to hear a story? No one can stay sad as long as there are stories to be told."

"Yes. Please!" Ningiyuk's face brightened.

"I'll tell you a special one, about the sun."

"That should cheer her up." Okio came crawling through the snow doorway. "Can I listen too?"

"Only if you stay as quiet as an Arctic lemming," the old lady told her grandson.

"I will," Okio promised. He scrambled around on the snow platform until he found Itow's special fur pillow. Then she was ready to begin.

3

The Story of the Sleepy Sun

"Many long years ago our ancestors came to this lonely Arctic island in search of happiness. No one knows exactly where they came from, nor how they got here. Some of our legends tell us one thing while other legends speak differently. But all agree that winter caught them by surprise, and the journey had been so hard that there could be no turning back."

"They wouldn't want to go back!" Okio was horrified at the thought.

"They must have—many times." The old lady smiled at him. "Since you were born here and have seen the sun return only eleven times, I wouldn't expect you to understand how strange and frightening it was for them. Without a tree in sight, they wondered how they could exist. Wild animals threatened their lives, and starvation was a constant fear. Instead of their land of dreams, they found themselves on a frozen desert. Legends tell us they kept looking back with longing in their hearts. It did them no good, for their footsteps were covered for all time."

"But there must have been seals and fish under the ice to provide them with food." Ningiyuk's heart was aching for her forefathers. "And surely they could catch ptarmigan and Arctic hare in the summertime?"

"Yes, child, the same wildlife was theirs. But breaking through walls of ice was so new to them. So, if both of you will stop interrupting me, I will tell the story as I heard it. And since we have no writing, we must hand the legends down with the words of truth in them." Itow shifted herself into a more comfortable position, then continued.

"Almost overnight our ancestors had to invent weapons to protect themselves from the wild animals. At the same time the women learned to carve dishes and tools out of the soft soapstone, which was in such abundance. It was an old man who invented the seal oil lamp. And since it provides us with heat as well as light, it is sometimes called a stove. But whether called a stove or a lamp, it is still the most prized possession in our igloos.

"As it is now, the main food was seal and fish. Like us, they had to wrestle with the waters and then the ice to get it. When the stormy blasts came, they had no choice but to dig into the drifts for shelter.

"One day a hunter was caught in a storm and there was no drift thick enough to crawl into. Rather than freeze to death, he carved snow blocks from the packed snow with the copper knife he had made for himself. Very carefully he placed the blocks around himself, and then in a circle he built them up over his head."

"That would be the first igloo!" the children exclaimed. Okio laughed until his sides were sore. Not even in his imagination, could he think of a world without igloos.

"That is true. And we've been living in them ever since," the storyteller went on. "But just as they were getting used to their new way of life, a sad thing happened to them. They found this harder to bear than the bitter cold weather.

It was worse than their hunger pains, and even the howling of the wolverine was as nothing in comparison. It—"

"Whatever was it?" Okio interrupted. A cold fear was creeping over his head and down his neck. His hair bristled.

"It was the strange action of the sun. Never before had they seen the great light get weary and go into hiding. The people were fearful that the sun spirits had been offended. There was terror on their faces as they watched it rise later each day and go to bed earlier each night. Then, one day it slept in until noon without as much as saying, 'I'm sorry,' or 'Good-bye.' It simply dropped out of sight, and they were left in darkness. By this time the people were frantic with fear. They offered every known sacrifice to please the spirits. But the angry darkness hung over them like an evil omen.

"Of course, the moon and the stars did their best to take the place of the sun. But our ancestors could not accept the pale light. Even the bravest of the hunters were fearful. Instead of going out to the hunting grounds, they stayed close to their igloos and fished through holes in the ice for tomcod. They were barely able to exist, but worse things were to come. The fish refused to bite and the darkness grew blacker. The people crowded inside their igloos and waited."

"What were they waiting for?" Ningiyuk's heart was thumping so hard, she was afraid Okio might hear it.

"I don't think they knew themselves what they were waiting for. They had lived in darkness for almost three months, and life had become unbearable. They thought they would rather face death than go on living without the sun. Then, one day, a little girl stirred in her sleep and called out, 'The sun! It's back! I saw it in the sky!'

" 'You've had a bad dream. Go back to sleep.' Her parents tried to quiet her. But the child was wide awake. She kept on shouting, 'The sun! The sun!'

"Quickly all the children in the large igloo awakened, and a joyful song filled their snow house. 'The sun is back. The sun! The sun!' They clapped their hands and jumped up and down with joy. On went their clothing and outside they went. From igloo to igloo the good news was spread. The children formed a procession and started for the hilltop. The grownups nodded their heads but followed at a distance.

"The sun *was* coming up! The whole southern sky was aglow. Golden beams reached out and touched the earth. The colors changed; and like magic, the sparkling white world was tinted pink. No one spoke. They scarcely breathed, for fear of disturbing the light beams that linked them to the heavens. Then, right before their eyes, the flaming sun floated up into the sky. 'Good morning, everyone!' it seemed to say.

" 'Good morning, our own beautiful sun! Welcome back!' the people shouted. They threw off their mitts so that the light could touch their hands as well as their faces. They clapped and they danced. All joined hands and around and around the big heap of mitts they danced with the sunbeams sparkling on the snow. Their fears vanished in the light of the sun, and joy was in their hearts."

"The sun still brings joy," Ningiyuk's eyes were starry bright, "and we greet it the very same way."

"Let Grandmother finish the story," Okio was impatient to hear the ending.

"The story has a happy ending." The old lady smiled. "The return of the sun brought new life and hope to the people. The hunters went back to their hunting, and the women returned to their igloos with a song in their hearts. But happiest of all were the children. They had believed deep in their hearts that the sun would come back. Never once did they give up hope. And just as they believed, it has returned every spring to this very day."

"That was your best story—ever." Okio looked at his grandmother with new respect.

"But remember this well." The old lady put up her warning finger. "The sun spirits must never be offended. The sun holds a strange power. It is stronger than the mightiest hunter."

Okio pretended not to hear. He finished eating a frozen fish and tried to persuade his sister to go outside.

"No. I want to talk with our grandmother. There are many things I can learn from her." Ningiyuk wriggled closer to the old lady's side.

4

Ningiyuk's Folklore Song

"Do dreams *really* come true? They must!" Okio was scarcely out of hearing when Ningiyuk asked urgently.

"I'm an old woman. Some people say I am wise. It would be foolish for me to try to answer your question. I haven't that much wisdom."

"But the girl in your story had a dream. And it came true!" A wistful expression came over the child's face. "Perhaps if I wish hard enough?"

"You dream and wish too much," her grandmother scolded. Then she picked up her *ooloo* and began scraping skins. "Sometimes dreams come true, and sometimes they don't come true."

Ningiyuk sat thinking. Her own special dream about the lovely lady would surely come true. *I'll make a wish on every star! And if I were a boy, I'd go in search of her.* Many thoughts went racing through her troubled mind. *I won't give up. There must be a way.*

"Many times I have heard you say that Eskimo people are only happy in their own tribe. Where is happiness to be found when you are adopted and taken away from your tribe?" Her voice was quivering with emotion. She dare not ask the old lady whose child she was.

"You were hurt yesterday, because Okio talked too soon." Itow was filled with pity and understanding. "Babies are different from grownups, for their happiness is found where they are loved and fed. You are one of us now. And your hurt will pass."

After a long silence Itow spoke again. Her voice was agitated. "Forget about being adopted, child. But never forget to please the spirits, especially the spirits of the sun." With her warning finger held high, she added, "It frightens me to think what will happen if we forget the beliefs and the rites of our ancestors." She was trembling from head to foot.

Ningiyuk pulled away from her grandmother. Such talk made her feel chilly and uncomfortable. But her heart melted when she looked into the brown leathery face. Her grandmother always meant so well. "We're not a very happy pair, are we? I'm sad because I'm adopted, and you're filled with fears because of the things you believe. My father says you are bound with the chains of paganism."

"They are the chains my ancestors gave me. And the chains of my choice!" Itom spoke sharply. "But if you have no fears of the Great Spirit you are learning about, should there not be a smile on your face, even though you know you are adopted?"

"Yes, there should be a smile on my face," Ningiyuk admitted. "But I'm sad about something else. I keep remembering that the sun will soon be gone. Can anyone be truly happy in the long darkness?"

"Of course!" Itow made it sound so simple. "You can pretend the igloo is your world, your happy igloo world."

"That could never be." Ningiyuk shook her head.

With one of her mysterious smiles, the old lady pointed to the seal oil lamp. "There is your sun, for does it not give us our light and heat? And above," she pointed upward, "we have a sky that is made from snow blocks. As you can see, they aren't pretty and blue. But when the igloo was new, it sparkled like a million stars; and the ceiling stayed fresh and bright long after the walls were soiled and dirty."

"And I suppose the snow floor is the earth?" Ningiyuk's imagination began to work.

"Yes, of course, this half that is raised is the earth. It supports us while we sleep at night, and I sit on it all day long. The sea is below us." She looked at the lower half of the floor. "And there are the fish and seal to prove it!" They both laughed at the sad-looking pile of frozen fish and seal meat.

There were other things to compare—like the fox pelt which hung on the peg that was stuck in the snow wall. And there were caribou legs propped against the drying rack that was built over the seal oil stove. They were the wild life.

"It *is* a little igloo world." Ningiyuk felt more content.

But outside, it was just as she knew it would be. The days grew shorter and shorter. The people seemed to be racing with the fading daylight to get much work done before the darkness. Okio helped his father saw ice slabs from the freshwater lake. They hauled the huge slabs down near the igloos. Instead of a well or running water, they had their ice pile! Together, they covered many storage places of fish and seal meat more securely to hide them from the wild animals that were always on the prowl.

Then one day the sun vanished completely. "It has gone to sleep," one old man nodded sadly.

"Ah yes. It must get very weary," the people agreed. Silently they went back to their igloos.

Ningiyuk was weeping. The darkness folded over her like a black fishnet. It weighed her down so, her feet dragged as she headed back home. When she knelt beside her grandmother for comfort, her eyes were swollen.

"There's no need for tears, my child," Itow said. "I've been busy making up a folklore song for you. I just finished it when you went out to bid the sun good-bye."

"But I haven't earned a folklore song! What brave deed have I ever done?" she asked, through her tears.

"It's for you, just the same. Now sit down and listen while it's fresh on my mind."

Ningiyuk was bewildered. But she sat down as she was told. With wide open eyes she listened to her folklore song.

> Today the sun dropped out of sight.
> I waved and waved then waved good-night.
> The brave good sun tried hard to say,
> "I'm not coming back for many a day."
>
> I shed some tears; it's all so sad.
> When the sun's away, I feel so bad.
> Outside it's cold; I'd be sure to freeze.
> So, into the igloo I crawled on my knees.
>
> The grownups listened to my tale of woe.
> "Be glad," they said, "for this house of snow.
> It shelters you well. The stars are above.
> There is heat and light, and lots of love."
>
> Then I knew in a flash I'd been mistaken.
> The sun was gone, but I wasn't forsaken.
> I'll laugh and sing, I'll brighten the days.
> To others around me, I'll be the sun's rays.

"You have spoken the feelings that are deep in my heart." Tears came streaming down Ningiyuk's cheeks. "But how could you know my feelings?"

"I was a girl once." The old lady smiled. "It's strange how I can't speak these things without feeling foolish. But like my ancestors I speak my best thoughts in a folklore song."

Ningiyuk looked with wonder at the old woman. It was very hard for the little girl to understand how anyone who was always on guard against evil spirits could have such lovely thoughts. Besides, Itow was old and wrinkled. "I'll learn the folklore song by heart," Ningiyuk promised. "And some day I'll pass it on to my grandchildren."

But her grandmother seemed not to hear what she was saying. Her thoughts were again in the past. Fresh in her memory were the many times she had watched the sun disappear, although the days of her childhood had been many years ago.

5

Koko and the Blizzard

Ningiyuk did learn the folklore song—every word of it! And she didn't let herself stay sad, especially in the daytime. Each morning when the igloo chores were finished, she played with the other children under the light of the moon beside the igloos. Some of the sparkle came back to her eyes, and the paleness left her cheeks.

But at night, before sleep would come, she recaptured her lovely dream. The beautiful lady was always there, as clear in her imagination as in her dream. Each night she made fresh plans for finding the lovely lady. *She was in a crowd; so, one day I'll find her in a crowd. Maybe at the Christmas celebrations!* Ningiyuk began counting the days until they would leave their igloo village behind and go to the white settlement for Christmas.

Like the wind in a blizzard, her thoughts kept changing about the secrets of her past. Why did my parents give me away? was always the last question on her mind before falling asleep.

Not long after the family had settled into the routine of the dark cold days, Komoyiok announced that he must replenish their supply of seals. Looking toward his son, he ordered, "Get yourself ready. We'll be starting for the sea ice tomorrow."

Okio sprang from the snow platform in one big jump. "I'm a man now! My father takes me hunting in the dangerous season." Excitedly, he began to make preparations.

After the man and the boy had left on their hunting trip, life in the igloo was very different. There seemed always to be a strange fear hanging over the white dome, and the days passed slowly. Itow was on guard for strange sounds, especially the howling of wolves. Atuk kept poking at the moss wick in the seal oil stove. It burned and spluttered, but still she kept poking. Ningiyuk had waved a happy good-bye to the hunters. She was glad to be rid of Okio and his teasing, but before many days she became lonely and restless. She longed for their return.

"Do you hear them coming?" Ningiyuk asked excitedly. The old lady was listening to something. Her ears were against the snow wall.

Itow's face was pale. "I hear the whining of the wind. It gives warning that a blizzard comes quickly!"

"A blizzard!" In seconds Atuk and Ningiyuk had their double fur garments on and were outside. The arctic blizzards often lasted for several days, and they had to bring in the food and seal oil to keep them alive and warm. Already the storm was raging, and they had to join hands for safety. When they reached the nearest fish storage place, it was difficult to uncover. Finally, Atuk loaded one of the child's arms and urged her to hold fast with the other hand to the rope that led back to the igloo.

Somehow, while Ningiyuk was going back and forth with fish, Atuk managed to uncover a *pok-sac* of seal oil and to grasp a slab of ice as well. Staggering against the stormy blasts, she shouted to Ningiyuk to get inside. The blizzard was becoming worse.

"Not yet!" Ningiyuk's voice could scarcely be heard. "Koko has to be brought into the igloo."

"No! No! Dogs have fur to keep them from freezing. *Come back!"*

But Ningiyuk didn't hear. She dropped the rope and ran headlong into the storm. The howls of her favorite husky were her guide. All the way down the dogline she groped her way, taking short gasping breaths as she went. Finally she reached Koko. Without removing her mitts, she unsnapped the chain and clung to the dog's collar. Together they raced to the safety of the igloo.

"Father Komoyiok asked me to take care of her." Ningiyuk flopped on the snow bench. "I had to bring her in."

"Never! Never did your father intend that you should risk your life!" Atuk sat weakly beside the breathless child.

"What a foolish girl," Itow scolded. "The husky soon would be sheltered under a snowdrift."

"It's a big blizzard." Ningiyuk began making a fur bed for the dog. "And Koko would starve, for sure."

The two older women began at once to prepare for the stormy blasts. They checked their supplies and examined the snow blocks for chinks. No one felt like talking. Ningiyuk crawled into bed to keep warm and to sleep.

But whether they were awake or asleep, the storm was a thing of terror to them. It whirled and whined outside the snow wall. And its terror seemed to have the strange power of reaching inside the igloo! Behind every object there lurked black shadows that looked like wild animals. Every time the seal oil lamp spluttered, the fearsome shadows leaped upwards, as if to attack. Outside the whine of the wind was weird and strange.

"Our walls are so thin!" Ningiyuk cried out. She knew

that if the blasts should break through, she and the women would freeze like icy statues.

"The walls may be thin, but they are strong." Itow was at her side. "Eat some of this fish and you'll feel better."

Time and time again, Ningiyuk awakened from her sleep. The storm raged in her ears, whether awake or asleep. About the fifth day she awakened suddenly and thought the blizzard was past.

"It's worse than ever," Atuk told her. Deep fear was written all over her mother's weary face. Her eyes looked like sunken pieces of coal. Only a few times had she allowed herself to doze since the storm began.

"You look sick." Ningiyuk offered her the last morsel of food in the igloo.

Atuk shook her head. "Eat it yourself. My hunger pains are gone."

"Neither am I hungry." Ningiyuk looked toward her grandmother. With tenderness in her heart, Ningiyuk threw the fish across the igloo.

But Koko leaped up and snatched the flying food. In one gulp it was gone. The women shook their heads in despair. There was nothing they could do now but wait— and hope.

Ningiyuk tried her best to fight against sleep. She wanted to keep guard with the two exhausted women. But the storm drowsiness came over her, and she drifted away.

"Wake up! The storm is over!"

The words rang clear in Ningiyuk's ears. She rubbed her eyes and turned in her sleeping bag. *Another dream,* she thought. Then she heard Koko snarl. She blinked and sat straight up. Out of bed she bounced towards Koko. But only so far, for the dog's teeth were bared.

"Koko has pups!" She squealed with delight. "One—two —three—there's five of them!"

"Yes." Atuk's face was crinkled with a smile. "The blizzard did its worst, but we weathered it, huskies and all." But deep lines of worry returned to her leathery face. "There can be no peace in my heart until our men return. The storm came without warning."

"Father Komoyiok has the power to feel a storm in his bones, even before there are signs." Ningiyuk touched her mother's shoulder.

But some of the happiness of their own safety and the thrill of the new pups left Ningiyuk as she did the igloo chores. She tidied every inch of their igloo and lastly sprinkled a carpet of white snow over the floor. Their hunger pains gave them no peace, but no one complained. Ningiyuk sat with the women and scraped skins. For hours they sat without speaking a word.

Then Itow put her ear to the snow wall. "I hear a dog team in the distance. It can be none other but our own!"

Ningiyuk ran outside. She blinked, for her eyes weren't used to the starlit whiteness. Then she saw a black moving speck in the whiteness. Without asking permission, she bounded over the drifts to meet them. "I've a surprise for you. Koko has pups—five of them!" she called out breathlessly.

"So have we a surprise," Okio shouted back. "We have seals—five of them!"

The team paused, and Komoyiok pulled Ningiyuk up beside him on the sled. "It seems you have looked after Koko well." He patted her head. "And I had no need to worry about the women in our igloo."

"But we're all so hungry. Terribly!" She rubbed her stomach.

"Mush! Mush!" Komoyiok whipped the dogs. "Home—and a feast!"

That night everyone ate to their heart's content. Then after the feast, drowsiness came over them. They staggered to their sleeping bags and slept for a night and a day.

6

An Arctic Christmas

After the seal hunting trip, the men paid a lot of attention to their trapping. The thick, glossy pelts would be traded for the few necessities they needed from the trading post. Christmas was only weeks away. They knew this because each family had been given a piece of paper with as many marks as there were days until Christmas. After each sleep they checked off one mark. At Christmas the white folks would give them another paper that would tell them when to return for Easter.

"Let's leave early to go to the white settlement," Ningi-yuk coaxed her father. Whenever she thought of the many people gathering in from all the tribes, her heart would skip a beat. *Perhaps?* She dared to hope.

"That's a good idea!" Okio agreed with his sister for a change.

Komoyiok did not seem to hear his children. But Atuk's steel cold eyes rebuked them. "We will leave when your father says we will leave. Not before."

It was always the same. The women and children were not to know the plans of the the men. But, in silence, every family was preparing for the departure. Then one bitterly cold day, each man announced in his own igloo, "Today we will leave to celebrate Christmas in the white settlement."

39

With much excitement and hurry they piled all their belongings on top of the huge family sleds. Carefully, the strong tarpaulins were lashed with sealskin ropes to hold things secure. Then, midst the howling of the huskies, the children were thrown high onto the loads. Dog whips cracked over the backs of the teams. "Mush! Mush!" And the teams galloped off.

"Our poor snow village. It looks so lonely without people in it." Ningiyuk waved from their sled as they pulled away. "Tonight it will be a home for wild animals. And in the spring it will melt away."

"That is life," said her grandmother.

"But sometimes I wish we could stay in one place, like the white people do."

"You silly child!" Komoyiok was listening. He couldn't visualize such an existence. "We must follow the ways of our ancestors, for they were wise. In the springtime we naturally move out to the sea ice just as it begins to break up. The seals are in abundance, and we build storage places filled with the precious meat. But when summer comes, our people must be near the river mouths. They are filled with fish for a short time. We need to be there to get a good supply."

"And we'd starve to death, if we ever tried staying in one snow village all winter." Okio chuckled. "Even a girl should know that the foxes get wise and move beyond our trap lines. Besides, the bears and the animals are wanderers. We have to keep on the move for good hunting."

"You are *so* wise." Ningiyuk said crossly.

But it wasn't a time for quarreling or sadness. The children jumped off the sleds to run alongside over the drifts. The adults shoved them away when they tried to get back

on. Laughter and tinkling sleigh bells echoed back and forth in the crisp air. They sang songs about the moonlit snows as the sleds drifted over the whiteness.

Building their small overnight igloos was more fun than work. "They are fairy castles!" Ningiyuk and her friends danced, in turn, around the eight sparkling igloos as they were quickly made. Like magic, they changed to golden domes. The seal oil lamps had been lighted. It was time to go inside and sleep.

After the third sleep they arrived at the settlement. The white sloping hills were alight with golden domes, for many people had arrived ahead of them. They greeted each other with warm embraces and handshakes. Within an hour many friendly hands had helped Komoyiok build their Christmas home. Then the visiting began! "Ah, it is good to be together," the people kept repeating over and over.

Ningiyuk left the children, who gathered in the largest igloo to play, and made the visiting rounds with her parents. Her searching eyes missed no one. But the lovely lady was not to be found. *Perhaps on Christmas day?* She was full of hope.

There were only three white homes in the settlement. In turn, they visited the Hudson Bay Company home, the Royal Canadian Mounted Police barracks, and the mission house. At each place they received warm hospitality and a steaming mug of hot tea. Then they returned to their igloos, and the visiting continued. When their eyelids were so heavy that they could no longer lift them, they went to bed and slept right through until Christmas Eve.

Everyone had new fur outfits to wear for Christmas. The children strutted back and forth to be admired. But the grownups were very casual, pretending not to notice the finery of the clothes parade.

Under the pale light of the moon each family trudged in single file toward the mission. The huskies looked like fur balls as they lay curled up under the stars. There were hundreds of them dotted over the hills, and they were as silent as the night.

Mr. Jones, the young missionary, met each man, woman and child with a handshake. His happy wife stood at his side. The Eskimos thought that she must be ill, for her skin was very pale. But it was her hair that attracted each eye in wonder. Never had they seen hair that was the color of the golden flame above the seal oil lamp!

The chapel filled to overflowing, and many crowded into the adjoining house. There was standing room only, even in the two small bedrooms. Mrs. Jones played music from the strange little organ. It was Christmas music. Then the missionary told the Christmas story in a way that the people could understand. This is how it was.

> Many long years ago Mariak was to become the mother of God's (the Great Spirit) Son. It was a secret that she and her husband, Josepuk, held deep in their hearts.
>
> Even so, they had to make a long journey to the south, for the chief of many tribes had ordered all the people to report to him. He not only wanted to count their numbers but demanded that each man leave him a gift. From the mighty hunter he would ask for a bearskin. But the usual donation was a fox pelt. The very poor had to leave only some frozen fish.
>
> It was a long tedious journey. Josepuk walked beside the sled all the way and guided it carefully over the rough places. Sometimes Mariak walked as well. The load was heavy, as they carried supplies for the journey.

When at last they reached the big settlement, **Mariak** was exhausted. She knew her baby would soon be born. "Do you think that anyone would be kind enough to let us share their igloo for the night?" She looked at the many igloos on the hillside.

"I'll build you an igloo with my own hands." Josepuk smiled at his young wife. "The blocks will be pure and white, and it will sparkle like the stars above."

"But there isn't time," Mariak whispered softly. "We must accept help from whoever is kind enough to give it."

Josepuk quickly unhitched the dogs. He took Mariak by the arm, and they presented themselves before the big chief. Many people were ahead of them, and each man was asked about his hunting success.

"Please!" Josepuk spoke above the loud talk. "Could someone let us share their igloo for the night? My wife must have a place to stay."

"Go to the next igloo. There you will find men to build an igloo," the chief spoke sharply. He resented the interruption.

Josepuk and Mariak left. The next igloo was filled with people. They were dancing to the rhythm of the sealskin drum. "Help me!" Josepuk asked over and over, but no one seemed to notice him.

From igloo to igloo they went. But it was celebration time for the people. All were too occupied to listen. Finally one old man, when he looked into Mariak's gentle eyes, took pity on them. "You are welcome to go into the little igloo that is built into our snow tunnel," he told them.

"But there are pups in that shelter! We passed them on our way in," Josepuk protested.

"All the better to keep us warm." Mariak smiled gratefully at the old man. "Come, Josepuk. We have found a place for the night."

Josepuk made Mariak a bed of furs. The puppies nestled at her feet. Before morning the baby was born.

Mariak wrapped Him in the softest furs and laid Him on the snow bench. Many people passed by the snow tunnel as they went in and out of the igloo. But they scarcely noticed the event that had taken place.

But there were watchmen out on the hills, who were outside the settlement. They were on the lookout for prowling wolves, when they saw strange lights in the sky. Now these were brave and mighty men; but when the lights came down, they trembled with fear.

Then voices broke through the light and the watchmen were the first to hear the good news. "Jesus, the Son of the Great Spirit, has been born. He comes to bring love, and joy, and peace."

The men lost their fears. They ran all the way to the settlement. With no difficulty, they found Mariak with the baby. When they spread the news, the people were speechless. "Why, oh, why were we too busy celebrating to welcome the child of the Great Spirit?" Many women hurried to be with Mariak and the baby.

There also appeared in the sky a bright glowing star. It shone above the igloo where Jesus was born. Some great and wise chiefs came from far away to bring gifts and to worship the baby.

One of the chiefs brought a big pok-sak of seal oil. Another chief brought his best furs and laid them at the feet of Mariak and the child. A third one brought the best food he could find. There was plenty for everyone. All the people who came brought their love.

A hushed silence had fallen over the mission. When the Christmas story was told, the people stood in awed reverence. Then, together they echoed the words, "And they all brought their love."

7

Winter and the Lights

Christmas lasted for many days. The people went back time and time again to the mission. "Jesus is one of us," they said, remembering the Christmas story. And they felt a great desire to learn more about Him.

But, as in previous visits to the mission, some of the old folks refused to hear the message. "How can you learn if you refuse to listen?" Ningiyuk begged her grandmother.

"Leave me as I am. I'm too old to change." Itow would shake her head sadly.

But the Bible stories were told and retold in the igloos, and the hymns were sung until the people knew them by heart. Komoyiok began to pray to the Great Spirit. He and Atuk would kneel with their children around the light of the seal oil lamp. They had been freed from the fears of the evil spirits, and there was peace in their faces. Itow sat silently on the snow bench. Her face was like a soap-stone carving with deep-carved wrinkles and haunted eyes.

Finally it was time for trading. Komoyiok's family had been waiting restlessly for several days. At last he gave the signal. He threw the large bundle of pelts over his back and began complaining. "It shames me to face the trader. These pelts are so poor and scruffy that he may not want to look at them."

46

"Indeed, no!" his family assured him. "You said the same thing last year. But your furs are the best there are. We are all so proud of your hunting skills."

They started on their way to the trading post. As always, Komoyiok's family walked behind him at the proper distance.

The trader gave them a hearty welcome. After shaking hands with each one, he apologized for the lack of heat. The store was much colder than their igloos. "Even our conversation freezes out here," was his favorite joke.

"Are those frozen words?" Ningiyuk pointed to the gray, unfriendly cloud that hung over them.

"That's our breath!" Okio was embarrassed. He motioned to his sister to stay in the background.

But none of them felt the cold. Trading was the most exciting thing in their lives. The trading post was one large square building with shelves lining three walls. The shelves were filled with trade goods. Each box held a special mystery for Ningiyuk, and her bright eyes tried to penetrate them all.

Komoyiok threw his large bundle on the floor. Then, one by one, the pelts were handed over the counter. In exchange he asked for ammunition, fish nets, and fox traps. A goodly supply of tea, sugar, and tobacco was piled beside them.

Atuk's needs were flour and baking powder for her bannocks. She then asked for a roll of bright calico, and braid for trim. This was to make a gay covering for their single outfit of fur worn in the summer. Many people had to do without, but not the family of Komoyiok, the mighty hunter.

Grandmother Itow wanted some curved steel needles.

"To help my old stiff fingers make finer stitches." Just recently she had stopped using the bone needles of her own making. After some hesitation, she pointed to a bottle of perfume.

Neither Ningiyuk nor her brother were allowed free choice. But after a nod passed between Komoyiok and the trader, Okio was handed a hunting knife. He dashed outside to show it off.

From the top shelf a box was brought down for Ningiyuk. It was a doll! The most beautiful one in the store! Her dolls always had been made from fur pieces. Ningiyuk hardly knew what to do with this one. Very gingerly, she stroked the golden hair, and the strange feeling passed. Then she scooped it up in her arms and hugged it to her young heart. Without even thanking the trader, she ran out excitedly. "Look! A real doll!" she called out for everyone to hear.

There was so much excitement in the settlement that no one listened to her. Many sleds were leaving to go back to their hunting grounds. Huskies were howling and pulling on their traces. Children were squealing and running hither and yon. Suddenly Ningiyuk saw something that made her gasp with joy and surprise. Near one of the loading sleds a beautiful lady dressed in white furs stood out from all the other people. Her eyes were searching for someone!

"I'm here! I'm here!" Ningiyuk's heart pounded against her ribs as she raced toward the lady. She almost knocked the woman over.

"Whatever do you want, child?" The lady was annoyed as she struggled to keep her balance.

Ningiyuk stood speechless. It wasn't the beautiful lady

in her dreams after all. "I'm sorry. I thought I knew you," she mumbled.

"Here, take your doll." The lady picked it up from the snow where it had fallen in the collision. Another child appeared. He took his mother's hand, and they went toward the departing sled.

Hot tears flowed down Ningiyuk's cheeks. They froze and fell like tiny icicles to the snow. Her head ached, and she again felt a strange soreness come over her heart as she watched the sled vanish into the distance. She clutched her doll and whispered into the golden hair, "Perhaps at Easter."

The next day Komoyiok and his group left the settlement. As usual their farewells were brief. "We always have such loud hellos, but our good-byes are so quiet," the children remarked as they started off.

"That is our way," they were told without any explanation.

They were heading for the Ekaluktuk (big fish) river. There they would hunt and trap until ice break-up time when the river would be filled with fish!

A whole new snow village sprang up near the river as soon as they arrived. By bedtime all felt quite at home in their new environment. But with the Christmas festivities over, the days seemed longer and colder and darker than ever. The winter drowsiness came over the grownups and they scarcely left their sleeping bags. It was hard to speak without yawning.

But the children would have no part of hibernation! "It's storytelling time!" they declared and went from igloo to igloo. First they crowded around Operlak, who long ago had lost count of his years.

He had to keep blinking to stay awake. Even so, he told them legends of their ancestors, of the land, and of the sea. They listened as though they were hearing his stories for the first time.

After many other storytellers had done their part to satisfy the children's listening ears, it was Itow's turn. Dreamily, she told them stories of the northern lights. They stood speechless, for in some strange way she made them feel there was a mystery attached to the heavenly colors.

"Pay attention to them," she gave warning, "for they are full of messages. Soon they will appear to assure us that the dark days are coming to an end."

The children rushed outside, hoping to find them in the sky. But all they could see was the pale light of the stars and the moon.

Some nights later Ningiyuk and Okio went sliding on the river ice. Their voices rang out with laughter. Suddenly, both of them stopped and looked up. "The northern lights!" they gasped.

Like the whispering winds on the hill they had appeared. The sky was ablaze! On every sparkling star hung a rainbow of flaming color. There must have been music, for the flames began to dance! Back and forth across the sky they danced. Then they changed into flimsy curtains of light. Yellow, red, green, violet—the colors kept changing as they swished back and forth before the children's unbelieving eyes.

Then one delicate curtain of light separated from the others. It floated down and dipped low, almost to the earth. Okio reached out as if to touch the light. It was playful and teasingly tumbled far out of his reach. Then, on invisible wings, it went back to the heavens.

Together the children stood spellbound. Finally, the lights began to fade.

"The Great Spirit was there," Ningiyuk whispered.

"Yes, I know," Okio agreed. But neither of them felt like talking. When they did speak, it was in a whisper. Around and around the snow village they walked. Each one had a wish that the spell of the northern lights would stay with them—always.

8

The Sun and the Dance

"Keep watching for the return of the sun." Grandmother Itow would rouse from her daydreaming to remind Ningiyuk of the event.

"I am watching!" Ningiyuk's face brightened. "There is twilight in the southern sky. Every day it grows brighter. I know the very spot where the sun will come up!"

Every day she and her friend, Mituk, went to the hilltop and watched for the magic red ball to appear. "Surely it is teasing us," they decided, for the wait seemed so long.

But one day they came running back down the hill, shouting the good news. "The sun! The sun! It's coming back!"

Like bees swarming out of a hive, the people came out through their snow tunnels and followed the children to the highest hill.

Never had the newborn sun looked so good to them. It brought life back to their sleepy world. Rosy and bright, it looked down on the snows, and sunbeams reached out to tint the world with a soft pink glow. In the twinkling of an eye the sun turned to pale purple. Even the people took on a lavendar color. As the Eskimos watched in awe, the crystals in the snow suddenly glittered like gold.

"Welcome back!" someone shouted. The spell was broken.

They threw off their mittens, joined hands and danced in a huge circle around the heap of mitts. From the bottom of their hearts they sang the songs of welcome to the new sun. Never could their ancestors have sung more joyfully.

Somehow, with the sun touching her face and hands, Ningiyuk felt free as a bird. "I'm happy!" She danced wildly to the singing. She didn't care that she was adopted and her worries melted in the sunlight. Even her dream, that had followed her like a shadow, faded away in the distance.

But all too soon the sun-bathed world darkened. The sun dropped silently beneath the horizon, and golden beams chased after it. A hundred rays leaped out and arranged themselves in a fan formation. These messengers of the sun seemed to say, "I'll be back tomorrow and for many tomorrows to come!"

The people watched until the last rays faded, then plans for the big dance were made. The men began at once to build a huge igloo. It was the size of six igloos. Excitedly, the children watched the blocks being carved out of the drifts, then shaped, and skillfully fitted into place. Like a huge white mountain, the igloo arose before their eyes. Caribou skins were placed around the inner wall for seating and other comforts were provided. But it wasn't until the seal oil lamps were brought in that it became the place of the big celebration.

It was hardly finished when the people began to gather. The children came in first followed by the women carrying an abundance of food for the feast. They were followed by the menfolk. The last one to enter was Ahigiak with the great skin drum.

Since Ahigiak was the oldest among them, he was to lead in the dance. The people cheered him, but he didn't respond to their cheers. His shrunken weather-beaten body was frail, as well as old in years, and he tottered with weakness under the weight of the heavy drum. Slowly, he entered the circle. Still he didn't seem to notice the people around him; there was a faraway look on his face.

At last the large bone hammer was raised and the first boom rang out. With unsteady hands he began beating the drum, slowly at first. Gradually his strokes came faster and stronger.

He began to sing, "Ee-yah eeya. Ai-ya-ai-yah," to the rhythm of his strokes.

Suddenly his frailness left him. His body swayed back and forth with ease as his singing grew stronger. Soon all the people were singing and swaying, until the huge white dome echoed with their music.

Then strength like the wolf's came into Ahigiak! He held his drum high and began waving it around as though it were a feather. With the fury of the trapped bear, he hammered on it. His feet became nimble and he began to dance. His toes scarcely touched the snow floor as he danced the welcome to the sun. Then he sang a song:

> I'm old in years; it is no secret.
> The sun returned; I went to greet it.
> I'll dance and sing the whole night through.
> My folklore tales I'll share with you!

The people clapped and cheered. "Tell us about the

time you fought Nanuk (the bear) with your bare hands," someone called out.

"Ah, yes." Ahigiak threw off his *artigue* and held up his arms. On them were scars, as white as the teeth of the bear that had torn his flesh many years ago.

As though it had taken place only yesterday, the story began to unfold.

"It happened when I was barely a grown man, in the days before we had such things as guns. Ah, yes, the bow and arrow was our weapon then." The old man rubbed his brow in deep thought. "Many days of hunger we suffered, and when one is hungry he is driven to foolishness. Never was I so foolish as the day I fought the bear for wanting my seal." Ahigiak threw back his head and laughed.

"That seal I harpooned when experienced hunters were coming home with empty hands, day after day. Our people were almost starving. In my excitement I left the other hunters to hurry home with the good food. On the way I was challenged by a hungry bear. It was a matter of giving up that seal—or fighting the bear. I fought the bear!"

From then on it was as though the bear were in the igloo and the fight was taking place before their eyes. Ahigiak crouched low. There were both courage and fear in his eyes as the imaginary killer approached for the attack. With the agility of a young man, he sprang forward with the bone hammer grasped tightly. The tussle became a battle for the death of one, the hunter or the bear. Weird scraping sounds came from the drum. The people could almost feel the wild animal tearing the flesh of the man.

It was so real that the women closed their eyes and the children screamed with terror. But the eyes and the hearts

of the men were with Ahigiak as he fought for his life. Their own bodies felt the blows as the crazed animal tried to tear the man's body apart.

Then it was over. Super strength had come to the hunter's aid and the bear lay dying at his feet. A mirage seemed to cover their eyes for the skin drum looked like the bear. The old man sank down weakly beside his prey. He was limp and perspiring. The igloo was as silent as the sunrise.

Ahigiak hoisted the drum to a younger man then crawled to the edge of the circle. But the people put him back into the center. They clapped and praised him for his bravery. "The story of your life will become legend. Never will you be forgotten," the humble man heard them say.

All night long they danced and sang to the rhythm of the skin drum. One by one, the hunters told the tales of their brave ancestors, and the history of their people came alive. This was their time for celebrating. The sun was back!

9

Easter

Although the sun was back from its long winter sleep, the bitter coldness stayed with the people. But as the days grew longer and brighter, the snow village hummed with activity. The men set out longer traplines and went farther afield to hunt.

Inside the igloo, Grandmother Itow scraped the pelts with a new energy. Often she raised her *ooloo* to her mouth and ate the scrapings of fat. "It is good for my old body," she would say, chuckling.

The lady of the igloo worked far into the night. Atuk scarcely took time to sleep. Each member of her family would be wearing a new outfit for Easter. Never once did she have the furs tried on for a fitting. In true Eskimo manner, she took measurements by her eye. Ningiyuk's was finished first, and she squealed with delight when she saw it.

"Let me finish it." Itow ordered her to take it off. "These tails must be sewn on to protect you from the evil spirits."

"No! No!" Ningiyuk protested loudly. "We are taught that spirit chasers are foolish superstitions. The Great Spirit will protect me. I no longer believe—" She stopped short, for the old lady's wrinkled face was horror stricken. The

59

winter had not been kind to her, and in the light of the sun she looked pale and more shrunken than ever.

Ningiyuk removed the fur garment. She handed it over saying, "Sew the many tails on. They look pretty."

The days flew by, and once more the group of eight families were on their way to the white settlement. This time they were traveling in the sunlight. The greetings and visiting were even more enthusiastic in the springtime. As the children played with their friends in the sparkling world outside their igloos, Ningiyuk kept a watchful eye on all the adults as they came and went.

"Who are you looking for?" Okio asked her, impatiently.

"No-no one. I mean, no one y-you would know," she stammered.

"What do you mean? 'No one I would know,' " he insisted.

"That's what I mean," was all she would tell him.

Easter morning dawned bright and cold. "Come with us to the Easter service, please," all the family tried to persuade Itow. It was no use. She wouldn't come.

As at Christmas, the mission was packed. Everyone looked their best, dressed up in new furs. When the missionary began his teaching, they forget about their fine outfits. Except for the children, a hushed silence came over them. Why should the Great Spirit allow His Son, the man Jesus, to endure so much suffering? they wondered. They understood as the missionary explained.

"This was the payment for every one of us. It gives us the right to be called His children. And it gives us the freedom to enter the happy hunting grounds (heaven)."

"How do we please the Great Spirit?" one man asked

boldly. "What offering must we make when His anger comes down upon us?"

"God wants no offering except your love," the missionary told him. "The Great Spirit had so much love for us that He gave His Son as a gift to the world. The man, Jesus, made the sacrifice for all people. But after the payment was made, He went back to live with His Father." The people nodded with approval and understanding. Their teacher finished by saying, "Let us rid ourselves of our fears, and come to the Great Spirit with love in our hearts."

"He gave His Son for us!" They found it hard to believe that the Great Spirit was not an angry God. Many people gave their hearts and love to Him that Easter Sunday.

Ningiyuk had been standing beside her mother. Once when she looked up, she saw tears streaming down Atuk's face. It came as a shock to Ningiyuk. She had never seen the strong woman cry. She didn't think she knew how to cry!

After the service and the big Easter feast were over, Ningiyuk pulled her mother away from the crowd. She couldn't get the thought of those tears out of her mind. "Why were you crying in the church?" she asked bluntly.

Atuk hesitated. "Always I have thought it was a weak woman who cried. But today I wasn't ashamed of my tears." She took the child's hand and spoke softly, "Today I felt the closeness of the Great Spirit. The sun seems weak in comparison. Jesus' love softened my heart and the tears ran down."

Ningiyuk's black eyes filled with surprise. She had never seen such a gentle look on her mother's face. "But I thought you believed in the Great Spirit before, just like Father

Komoyiok does." She added with a twinkle, "And like Okio and I try to—even though we often forget the teachings."

"Yes, I believed," Atuk told her. "But mostly because Komoyiok told me I should believe. Today the Great Spirit came into my heart."

Ningiyuk wondered if her mother's face would stay gentle or if the harshness would return. A bigger surprise was in store for her.

"Easter Sunday is a good day to tell my secret. "Atuk's face seemed alight. She squeezed Ningiyuk's hand until it hurt. "Our family is to have a baby, come summer."

"Our family is to have a baby!" Ningiyuk echoed the words in unbelief. She didn't know why, but she started to cry.

"Run along and play. You're old enough to go sleigh-riding on the big hill." Atuk became embarrassed that so much emotion had passed between them.

Ningiyuk never had gone to the steep hill before. She dashed off and soon caught up to Okio. She helped him pull the sled, and hardly above a whisper she asked, "Did you know that there will be a baby in our igloo next winter?"

"Of course I know." Okio was quite casual. "And it had better be a boy!"

"You are so wise!" Ningiyuk was cross because he knew. "But you *should* be wishing for a girl."

"There's already one girl in our igloo. That's enough!"

"And what if that girl leaves your igloo? Who would wait on everyone and do the igloo chores?"

Okio stopped and looked at her. "Are you still thinking of your own parents? And your own tribe? Be content where you are."

"It was you who told me I was adopted. The yearning came then."

"You are one foolish girl," Okio told her.

They reached the top of the hill in time to see the first sled go swooping down. Others followed, one after the other. Each sled was piled high with children, and waving arms flew out in every direction. Now a spirit of competition entered the fun. They lined up in an even row at the top, then—swish! The sleds started off with a bumpety-bump and fairly flew to the bottom.

"It makes me think I'm a bird!" Ningiyuk laughed as she puffed her way back up the hill.

As time went on, the sleighriding became more hilarious and the children more daring. Suddenly the fun came to a stop. One of the larger sleds sideswiped Okio's, and there was a dreadful crash. Ningiyuk was thrown to the hard surface.

Over and over she rolled down the hill. Someone grabbed her near the bottom of the hill, but not before she struck her head on an ice-covered rock. She lay limp and silent, like a rag doll. Her face was almost as white as the snow.

Quickly, all the children gathered around. "Why doesn't she speak?" someone asked in a low voice.

"Hurry!" Okio began giving orders. "We've got to get her to our igloo."

The children stumbled about clumsily. But each one was doing his best to help. They wrapped her in caribou skins and placed her carefully on the largest sled. Then slowly and gently, they hauled her toward the settlement.

Someone had rushed to tell Komoyiok. He came running to meet them. After one look at the child, he pointed toward the mission. "We need the help of the missionary," he said.

10

The Great Spirit Above the Sun

With kind efficiency the missionary carried Ningiyuk into their home. "As you know, I am no doctor," he explained to Komoyiok, "but with the help of the Great Spirit, we will do our best for the child."

For the rest of the day a large crowd waited outside the mission to hear news of the sick one. They separated to let Atuk walk through. Courage was written over her anxious face. Soon, Itow was to be seen hobbling over the drifts, carrying a large leather pouch. It was her equipment for removing evil spirits.

"No! No! You can't practice your pagan rites inside the mission." The people tried to hold her back.

"And who is there among you that would stop an old woman from helping a sick child?" Her eyes were wild.

"Let Itow come in." The missionary's wife opened the door.

Itow got down on her knees and crawled inside. Since this was the first time she crossed the door of a white man's home, she entered the only way she knew how to enter a home.

Mrs. Jones took her arm and helped her to stand up. "Itow, you may stay here with Ningiyuk, but you may not use your spirit pouch." The missionary's wife spoke kindly but firmly. "We will pray to the Great Spirit and trust Him to make Ningiyuk well again."

For three days and nights the silent suspense continued. Komoyiok and Atuk came and went, but there were no words on their lips. Itow stayed at the child's side day and night. On the fourth day there was good news. It spread like the wind, from igloo to igloo. "Ningiyuk will live. She is almost well again!"

"Ah yes. The Great Spirit has listened to our prayers." The people were full of rejoicing.

"It is so," the missionary told them, "and tonight we will hold a service to thank the Great Spirit for the child's recovery."

"That is good." The people nodded. Later on they crowded into the mission with thanksgiving in their hearts. Itow was the first one there!

Unlike most old people, who for the first visit would hide themselves in the crowd, Itow sat on her crossed legs close to the altar. She looked tired and pale, but her face was peaceful. The fears had left her eyes! In her anguish for Ningiyuk, she had groped beyond the darkness and opened her heart. The Great Spirit had come in, and the chains of paganism were broken.

The people bowed their heads in great respect. Itow was old and wise, and she kept the legends of their ancestors before them. But could she give up the worship of the sun spirits? Many thoughts about her stubborn paganism ran through their minds as the service went on.

After the service, as if she read their thoughts, Itow raised her arm for attention and spoke. "You must think it strange that I am here. Somehow I don't feel like a stranger. For a long time Ningiyuk and others have tried to lead me to the mission. I thank you for your patience." She cast a smile to all the people. "But I was afraid of turning my back on the sun. Now, oh dear me—words are hard to speak. I'll tell you my feelings in a song. The words flew into my mind as I sat by the side of our sick child. Listen well, for it may be my last song. If anyone wants a name, it would be called, 'Beyond the Sun.'

> The sun is great. I know it well;
> It shines so bright, I feel its spell.
> But greater still, away up high,
> The Spirit of spirits is in the sky.
>
> He's down here too, on earth and sea;
> He's in my heart, I hope you see.
> I like the sun! It's still my friend,
> I love the Great Spirit to the end.

"So you see, I still have the sun; but having the Great Spirit in my heart makes the sun look small and pale." Itow looked around uncomfortably. No one had clapped at her song, and their silence made her feel embarrassed. "Could it be true that my words are not pleasing?"

"They are good words," the people told her. "They touch our hearts so deeply that anything we might say would sound foolish." There were tears in many eyes, but there was happiness in many hearts.

Another whole week passed before the missionary would allow Ningiyuk to leave the settlement. By this time the rest of the people had gone to their hunting grounds, but Komoyiok was careful to carry out the instructions for the safety of his child.

On their slow journey back, Ningiyuk entertained her family with tales of living in a white man's house. "It was just like being in another world," she explained. "And if only it wasn't as hot as a stewpot, I could have liked it."

"How could you sleep, since there were no snow platforms?" Okio wanted to know.

"I slept on a bed, you silly boy."

"And what is a bed?" he asked.

"You should have visited me when I was sick. You would have learned much," she told him importantly.

"I was afraid to," Okio admitted.

"Go to sleep!" Komoyiok ordered gruffly from his sleeping bag. "If we get a good start in the morning, we should arrive home by night."

Ningiyuk never knew such happiness as their return to friends and home brought. The children treated her as though she were somebody special—like a snow princess! "It's just me!" Ningiyuk laughed. "And I'm well again, even my cracked head!"

The sun shone down on the igloo village with such warmth that the igloos began to drip. "Let's move into our tents!" the children cried out in happy excitement.

But the adults shook their heads for the time had not come. They remedied the situation by cutting away the snow ceiling and throwing large tarpaulins on top the snow walls. *So now our home is half igloo and half tent.* Ningiyuk thought it an ugly sight.

It was only a few weeks until their skin tents were pitched on an elevated area. They lived in a brand new village. And for the next five months they would be tent dwellers.

Because of her accident, Ningiyuk was given much less work to do. Instead of resting, she roamed over the hills to feel and see the wonder of springtime. Water gurgled around the brown rocks in the streams and young Arctic hares leaped out from nowhere. Flocks of birds appeared in the sky and there was music in the air. And the sun! It never seemed to get weary anymore.

One day she saw a Canada goose. The huge bird with the long jerky neck was tiptoeing around the pond, proudly preening her feathers.

"I'll find your eggs, you poor goose!" Ningiyuk laughed.

The days flew by and summer came. The world was filled with sunshine, for the sun refused to set. Instead, it went around and around the sky in a great circle. It didn't even touch the northern horizon at midnight. The warmth caused the rivers to burst open, and it was fishing time. They would haul in tons of char.

"Ah, this is what we have been waiting for!" Komoyiok was ready with his huge sweepnet.

"It's nothing but *fish, fish, fish!*" Ningiyuk turned up her pug nose at the smell that was everywhere.

They ate fish for every meal. It hung on racks to dry, both inside and outside the tent. The dogs ate nothing but fish. Nanuk, the bear, came prowling around the tents for a meal of fish. The men worked day and night fishing and making storage places full of fish.

But the best part of summer was yet to come—the flowers! They were the wonder of the Arctic. Each one was a tiny miracle. They sprang out of the barren rocks with no soil, just from bits of moss hidden in the rough crevices. Their colors reflected the light of the rainbow, so varied and gay and bright. But, sadly, they were gone in a week or so, as suddenly as they had appeared.

At the height of their glory, Ningiyuk filled her arms with them and brought them to her grandmother. Then she went back for more.

It was a strange but beautiful sight to see the old lady sitting outside the tent, her lap filled with flowers. She sat looking at them for a long, long time. When at last she spoke, it was to the Great Spirit. "Let there be flowers in the happy hunting ground. And sunshine, please, to keep the flowers blooming forever."

11

Sealing and the Surprise

As always, the ice fields remained solid ice for a long time after the snow was gone. But they changed in appearance and became very exciting. Large ice cracks opened up, and seals would flop out of the icy waters. They loved the sun and would bask for hours in its rays.

The fish season was hardly over but the hunters were eager and anxious for an abundant seal harvest. It was their bread of life.

"We're going on an overnight sealing trip!" Okio announced to his sister. He added with excitement, "Father Komoyiok might let me do some of the shooting!"

"I'm going too!" Ningiyuk was as excited as her brother.

"You're a girl!" Okio thought she was joking.

"You keep reminding me of that." Ningiyuk's temper flared. "Father Komoyiok made many promises to me when I was sick. To go on a sealing trip was one of them." Off she went to ask permission.

Okio's face fell when she came back. "It's only because you were close to death that our father has turned soft." He turned and walked away. Over his shoulder he mumbled, "It just isn't right that a girl goes sealing. You've spoiled my day."

"I could be helpful." Ningiyuk tried to pacify him.

"I wouldn't know how."

The next morning the sled was piled high with harpoons and hunting equipment. Ningiyuk was sitting high up on the load. She waved gaily as the dogs galloped off at high speed. It wasn't long until their pace slowed down. The warmth of the sun had melted the surface ice, causing it to look like a great honeycomb. The sled was cutting through, making ruts as it went.

"It's beautiful, like icicles turned upside down," Ningiyuk exclaimed.

"Would you like to be walking on it on your bare feet?" Okio wanted to know.

"How right you are, my son." Komoyiok called the team to a stop. The huskies were beginning to limp. After examination, Komoyiok shook his head sadly. Their feet were tender and some were bleeding. He motioned for the bag of dog shoes to be brought.

"Oh, what a job!" Okio moaned at the sight of so many shoes. "Let me think. Eleven dogs means many, many shoes." Like his ancestors, Okio could not count beyond his fingers and toes.

"I think it's fun." Ningiyuk laughed at the large shoe pile. She began helping. The shoes looked like mittens without the thumbs. After each was slipped on a dog's foot, a sealskin lace was tied around the leg. It had to be tied firmly, yet not too tightly.

The dogs traveled much faster when their feet were protected. Sometimes a shoe became loose and fell off. The team was then stopped and the shoe was tied on more firmly.

"A seal! A seal!" Okio shouted. He pointed toward a black speck in the distance.

"This is your seal." Komoyiok threw a white covering over the boy's shoulder. "Remember what I have taught you. Act fast."

"Y-you don't mean I'm to g-go after it alone!" Okio stammered, hanging back. "It would bring bad luck to miss the first summer seal."

"Is that any way for a son of mine to talk?" Komoyiok's face was stern as he put the gun into the hand of the young hunter.

Of course Okio obeyed. He went in a great half-circle, to make sure the seal would not be shot back into the ice crack. While he was still quite a distance from the seal, he put the white covering over himself and got down on his hands and knees. It had looked so much easier watching his father. But courage came to him and he crawled forward, cautiously, slowly, never once taking his eyes away from the sleeping seal.

Then something aroused the seal's suspicion. He lifted his head high in the air and looked around in every direction. There was nothing to see. Okio was lying motionless as a lump of snow. The seal tucked his head under his flipper and fell asleep again.

Okio edged closer, ever so slowly. He wiggled forward by inches and was almost close enough to shoot. But the seal jerked his head up and again surveyed his surroundings. Everything was quiet and white.

"It's a game they're playing!" Tense with excitement, Ningiyuk watched every move from the distance.

"Shh—sh—sh." Komoyiok raised his hand to silence her. Okio was aiming his gun.

"Ping! Ping!" Okio rushed forward and pounced on the

struggling seal. He proudly stood guard until his father and sister arrived. He had shot his first seal!

Ningiyuk danced with joy. "You will be a great hunter, like our father!" It was the greatest compliment she could pay him.

"What's so exciting about shooting a seal?" Okio tried to sound as though he were used to shooting seals.

Komoyiok said not a word. But a strange new light, like the glow of the seal oil lamp came into his eyes as he looked at his son. He had dreamed of this day since Okio's birth. In silence, they loaded the seal on the sled and drove on.

This was a good hunting day, for they hadn't traveled far until they sighted and shot another seal. By camping time, three seals were on their sled.

It was fun preparing the meal in the tent, far out on the sea of ice. The two hunters ate in silence. Then Komoyiok began talking to Okio as though he were a man instead of a boy. Okio turned his back on his sister. Every time she tried to speak, he looked at her as though she were a foolish child.

He's trying to punish me for coming, she thought. *Besides that, his head has grown very large. He is now Okio the hunter!*

She crawled into her sleeping bag and listened to their conversation. Their voices grew distant. She was fast asleep. But frightening dreams disturbed her sleep. Okio was being mean and spiteful. He chased her onto the sea ice. A huge crack opened and she fell in. Her stuggling awakened her. What a relief to see her father and Okio sleeping peacefully in their sleeping bags!

But try as she would, sleep wouldn't come back. The

dogs were restless and tugged on their chains. One gave a warning snarl. Ningiyuk tiptoed to the door and opened the flap. To keep from screaming she clapped her hands over her mouth and ran to her father.

"Stay where you are, child," he ordered. In seconds he was dressed and dashed outside with his heaviest gun.

Ningiyuk was trembling with fright. She shook Okio

fiercely, but it was impossible to awaken him. "Let me sleep," he kept muttering crossly.

"BANG!" The great gun exploded outside the tent. It sounded as though the whole world was shattered!

Okio threw himself out of his sleeping bag. "What happened?" he kept shouting as he dressed and headed for the door.

"Don't leave me alone, please," Ningiyuk begged him.

"It's because you're a girl that you're frightened. Didn't I tell you—"

Komoyiok stood in the doorway. "It's lucky for us that the girl in our family came along. While we both slept, she heard the danger signals." He motioned for Okio to follow him. "See what she saved us from."

"A bear!" Okio gasped in astonishment. Then he hung his head in shame. He well knew that the bear would have stolen their seals and probably attacked the chained dogs. He began to apologize.

But Ningiyuk was too embarrassed to listen. She began to scold him. "Hurry up, and help Father Komoyiok skin the bear. I can't help. I'm only a girl!"

Komoyiok smiled proudly at both his children. "Yes, let's hurry. We have so much meat now, we'll have to make storage places on the land. We'll be kept busy for a long time."

"I can't wait to get home," Ningiyuk exclaimed, "to tell all the hunting news!"

"Just like a girl!" Okio said. He ruffled her hair good-naturedly, then went off to skin the bear.

12

Under the Midnight Sun

After much thought Ningiyuk decided not to talk about
her part in the bear episode. By the time they returned to
the settlement, she was as nonchalant about it as Okio was
about his hunting success.

"Our children are growing up," Komoyiok told his wife
when they were alone.

Atuk nodded. She didn't know his reason for saying so,
but it would not be proper to ask. The new pride she saw
in his eyes made her very happy. A husband who was
pleased with his hunting and family was the best reward a
woman could ask for. Life was being good to Atuk.

Soon after the sealing trip. Ningiyuk felt the lure of the
midnight sun and wandered away from the safety of the
settlement. "There's more magic in the sun at midnight!"
She danced over the rocks, with the hood of her single fur
artigue thrown back.

An Arctic hare appeared. It hopped from rock to rock
ahead of her, always keeping a safe distance.

"You think you're so clever because you wear a coat
exactly the color of the rocks," Ningiyuk scolded. "But
when the snow flies, you'll get back into your white coat!"
The world was full of wonders. She loved them all.

Around the ponds there were nests of different kinds and colors of eggs. They were concealed so well that Ningiyuk wondered how the birds could find them when they returned from searching for food. But they did. It was hatching time, so she left them undisturbed and went on to explore elsewhere.

After some time she noticed the sun was circling toward the east. It was long past midnight, and sadly she turned to go home. She walked and walked; then she began to run. *The settlement must be over the next hill,* she thought, frowning.

But it wasn't. Nor was it over the hill after that. Shivers ran up and down the child's spine. In every direction, as far as she could see, the tundra was strange and unfriendly.

With all the courage a ten-year-old could muster, she tried to recall the rules of getting lost. "I mustn't panic." She choked back a sob. "And instead of walking straight ahead, I should walk in a large circle."

Eagerly, she watched for someone to come looking for her, as she slowly traveled in a circle. But no one came. Her fears gave way to weariness. She sat down to rest just for a little while. Gradually, with the sun on her face, she curled up on the flat rock and fell fast asleep.

With a frightened start, she awakened. Koko was licking her cheeks!

Her heart leaped with joy. "You never forget that I rescued you in that blizzard, do you?" She threw her arms around the dog's neck, but Koko wanted no part of her affection. She snarled impatiently and headed homeward. Ningiyuk followed.

At first she thought Koko was playing tricks on her, for

they seemed to be going in the wrong direction. Then she sighted Okio. He was coming to meet them.

"Is my father angry that I wandered too far and got lost?" she asked fearfully.

"Were you lost?" Okio asked in surprise. "I doubt if anyone missed you."

Ningiyuk was taken back. Her temper flared. "I could have been eaten by wild animals! It seems no one cares if I'm lost or not."

"Koko must care." Okio laughed. "She was restless and pulling on her chain so much that I let her go free. And see what she found!"

"It's good to have a dog that cares!" Ningiyuk snapped back.

Okio could keep his secret no longer. "We have a baby in our tent. It's a boy!" he added triumphantly.

Ningiyuk looked at him wide-eyed. Her anger was gone. "I wanted a boy too!" she admitted. But it hardly seemed true that there was a baby in their tent.

"So now you can't leave our home." Okio was looking down at his feet. But out of the corner of one eye he was watching his sister's reaction.

There was none. Ningiyuk pretended not to hear. She turned and ran stumbling over the tundra to the tent to get a first glimpse of the baby.

"He's so—so beautiful!" she gasped when she gazed with wonder at the reddish brown, squirming babe.

"He looks exactly as Okio looked the day he was born." Atuk was feeling the grip of the baby's finger on hers. There was a tender glow on her tired face. The mighty hunter had two sons, and she was their mother.

Ningiyuk felt a stab of jealousy. "And me too? Surely he looks a little bit like me?"

Okio burst out laughing. "And you from another tribe! How could he possibly look like you, even a little bit?" He kept on laughing until he saw the harsh look on his father's face.

Ningiyuk's face was crimson under the brown. For several months she had hardly given a thought to being adopted. Even her dream, and the picture of the mother she searched for, was getting dim. "You would remind me!" She stamped her foot angrily.

"It's not a time for quarreling." Komoyiok couldn't conceal his happiness. "We must name the child."

Atuk looked toward her husband. All eyes turned to him, for the father would name his son. They waited for him to speak. "His name will be Kiyuk after my own father." Everyone nodded approval.

Itow let the skins she was scraping fall to the floor. After a long silence she said, "The child who bears my husband's name will be smiled upon by the Great Spirit. And he will surely be a mighty hunter."

Again there were nods of approval.

"But he sleeps so much!" Ningiyuk complained through the first weeks of his life. It seemed that he was either nursing or curled up sleeping in the pouch on his mother's back. Only in the evening was he taken out to be admired. "He's a kicker!" The children crowded close to watch him being exercised on soft furs. They squealed with delight at his antics.

Never, not even in her dreams, did Ningiyuk think it possible to love a tiny baby so much.

13

The Big Ship

The excitement of the new baby had hardly worn off, when Komoyiok announced that it was almost time to meet the big ship. They had decided not to break camp this year. Instead, the able-bodied would walk overland, using the dogs as pack trains. "This means the old people and the very young will stay behind. Somebody has to look after the pups." He looked straight at Ningiyuk.

"I'm neither very young nor a pup," Ningiyuk protested. "And I'm the best walker ever."

"You'd better get ready." Her father winked.

Ningiyuk was the youngest to go. This would be her first walking trip, and her excitement knew no bounds. She sang as she got ready, then everyone joined in the ship chorus:

> *Umiakpuk! Umiakpuk!*
> We'll be there to meet you!
> Umiakpuk! Umiakpuk!
> It's always fun to greet you!

All the hardships of the past year faded away at the thought of seeing the big ship. Besides, their Eskimo friends would be gathering from far and wide. *Perhaps this will be the time I find——.* Ningiyuk didn't finish her thought; her

82

mind was filled with a struggle. She didn't know what she really wanted.

In a few days they were on their way. With only a small bundle on her back, Ningiyuk leaped from rock to rock as gracefully as a caribou fawn. They crossed streams and passed a lake. Beyond each hill was a brand new horizon.

Ningiyuk was leading the procession. "It's fun," she called out. "Why don't we always travel this way?"

"You'll know by tomorrow," Okio answered back.

"Or tonight," others corrected him. Then laughter rang out. Some of them doubled up with glee and rolled on the rocks. "So our young one thinks this is a good way to travel!" They all laughed. It was reason enough to stop for a drink, so the solemn dog train was called to a halt.

It wasn't until midafternoon that Ningiyuk could understand their joke. Suddenly she did. Her rosy pink day changed to a dull drab one. Somehow her legs seemed shortened, for they could no longer keep up to the strides of the adults. Her cheeks burned from the glare of the sun and the breeze. But these things were nothing in comparison to the hot blisters on her feet. She could be brave no longer. "Has anyone filled my bundle with stones?" She moaned with the weight of her load.

This time the people didn't laugh. Someone picked the bundle off her back and carried it. Then two men hoisted her onto the back of Kituk, the strong one. For almost an hour he carried her as though she were a feather.

Finally, it was time to camp for the night. After eating their fill of dried fish and drinking from the stream, they spread furs on the rocks. The packs each one carried became their pillows.

Ningiyuk tossed restlessly. "Just for tonight I wish the sun would hide under a cloud."

But even at midnight the sun's rays shone brightly on their faces. Finally they covered their heads with light skins and slept until the sun had circled almost halfway around the sky.

The next day Ningiyuk's misery increased. "My bones are stiff enough to break. And look at my feet! They are swollen like two jellyfish," she exclaimed in horror.

But when she looked at the poor huskies, her own aches and pains seemed to vanish. The cruel jagged rocks were cutting their feet as they panted along with heads hung low. The heavy loads they carried seemed to be breaking their pride as well as their backs.

"Huskies always feel miserable on hot days, but being pack dogs on hot days makes them worse than miserable," she protested.

The people laughed at her concern. But she had more to say on behalf of the huskies. "I know what they would say, if only the poor animals could speak for themselves."

"Tell us, please!"

"This is what they would say," Ningiyuk spoke up bravely. " 'We are *not* your beasts of burden. We are the huskies of the north! And we are man's best friend!' "

"Well spoken," the travelers agreed. But they didn't laugh. "Let us celebrate the 'dog talk' by calling the dogs to a halt." So, at the first stream they unloaded their packs and allowed the dogs to run free for a spell. The huskies rolled in the cooling waters and drank to their heart's content. After that, much to Ningiyuk's delight, everyone treated the dogs more kindly.

Their journey took three sleeps; and when they arrived

in the settlement, many other tents already were pitched on the hillside. It was the same hill that had glittered with igloos at Eastertime. A day later, in the light of the midnight sun, the big ship came sailing up the bay.

"Umiakpuk! Umiakpuk!" echoed across the white settlement. People came running from every direction and lined up along the shore. They watched with awe as this yearly link with the white man's land floated toward them.

The policeman was wearing his bright red uniform—
which they hadn't seen on him since last Christmas. And
the rest of the white folks were wearing their finest furs.

Before the anchor was down, they all had piled into ca-
noes or rowboats. Then the race was on to see who could
be aboard the big ship first. Ningiyuk felt a little terrified.
She clung tightly to Okio and followed him like a shadow.
They found themselves on deck, jostled about by strange
elbows. Mugs of coffee were handed out—even to the
children. Everyone was talking at the same time. There was
news to be told from all along the coast, as well as from
the outside world.

Ningiyuk's shyness soon left her, and she ran with the
children up and down the decks. They explored the whole
ship and peeked into mysterious boxes.

"Their food tastes so horrid!" One little girl turned up
her nose at a lonely case of oranges.

"Yes, the white man has many strange ways," the other
children echoed the words of their parents.

"Come with me, child!" Komoyiok appeared suddenly.
His face was pale as he grasped Ningiyuk's arm.

Ningiyuk was filled with fright as her father half dragged
her to an empty cabin of the ship. Surely some dreadful
thing had happened. With all her heart she wished Okio
was with her, but Komoyiok had forbidden him to come.

Inside the cabin, Komoyiok sat on the floor and pulled
her down beside him.

"What have I done?" she asked fearfully.

"You have done nothing that is wrong," he told her.

Ningiyuk heaved a sigh of relief. "Then why do you
look so cross?"

"I'm not cross. I'm just—well—" He rubbed his furrowed brow. "Listen carefully, child. I have something very important to explain to you." His face turned paler than before as he added, "You have an important decision to make."

Ningiyuk's heart began flip-flopping inside her chest. How could she listen, she wondered, with such a loud hammering noise in her ears?

14

Back to Her Igloo World

Komoyiok began his explanation. "Almost a year ago, you learned that you were not our own child. And it made you feel sad. Many times your mother and I have seen you looking toward the west. There must have been a yearning in your heart to be with your own people."

"Yes," Ningiyuk agreed with great hesitation. Then the picture of the mother she had been searching for flashed in front of her. It could be that her dream was coming true! "You found my real mother? She's here in the crowd! Tell me everything!"

Her father looked up in surprise. "What gives you such a strange notion? Your own mother died the day after you were born. But just before she left for the happy hunting ground she gave you to us to be as our own child." His voice was low and sad.

"My mother is dead? She can't be!" Ningiyuk reacted to the news like a hurt animal. For a while she sat in a daze, staring into space. Komoyiok waited for her to speak.

Finally, she told him, "I had a dream. It was the night Okio told me I was not your child. In my dream there was a beautiful woman, and we loved each other. I was so sure it was my real mother."

88

The child could be brave no longer. She threw her arms around Komoyiok's neck and sobbed. "That dream has been my deep secret. All year I have been searching for her, and now you tell me my mother is dead!"

Komoyiok stroked her black shiny hair. "Dreams are dreams. But your mother was beautiful, and she would want you to think of her. Above everything else, she would want you to be happy." After a long pause he went on. "I want you to be happy too. That is why we must have this talk." Large drops of perspiration came out on his brow as he continued. "Your father is alive. He lives in the far west, near Aklavik. He sent a long message with the captain of the ship. He—"

"My father?" Ningiyuk interrupted him. *"You* are my father!"

"I can see now that I should have told you these things long ago. But I avoid soft words. Besides," he admitted uncomfortably, "I didn't want you to be thinking about your own people. You're such a little dreamer." There was affection in his brave eyes.

Ningiyuk was trembling with apprehension, yet she giggled. "Surely I must have been born, as Okio often tells me, without brains. Not once did I give any thought to another father. Always my father has been Komoyiok, the mighty hunter." Then her eyes implored him for understanding, "It was my dream that kept me thinking of another mother. Somehow, it helped me when I was feeling so sorry for myself."

"It is understandable," Komoyiok nodded. "But I'm here to tell you that your father is now a rich man. He has a wife and other children, and they live in a house like a white man's. If I am willing to give you up, he would pay me as many foxes as I would ask for raising you. He wants you to go and live with him." Komoyiok was looking down at the floor. Suddenly, he looked old and weary.

"He gave me away. And now he is trying to buy me back!" Her black eyes blazed with anger.

"It is not so," Komoyiok explained calmly. "Your parents were from the west of this island and were visiting our tribes when you were born. Your father had no choice but to give you away. He intended to return to his own people but was asked to work on the big ship on its journey west. I'd never heard from him until this day."

"He has no right to want me now."

"Your own father is offering you many things I can't give you—like going to school and speaking the white man's language. All the things you have been dreaming about can come true. You only have to say the word. The ship leaves in the morning."

"I won't say the word. I won't! I won't!" Ningiyuk stood up, screaming. "I belong to your family. You're sending me away!"

Komoyiok shook her roughly until her screaming stopped. "Such foolishness you talk! The truth is, I'd rather lose my arm to a bear than watch you leave on the ship. Our next meeting would be in the happy hunting ground."

"Then I'm not going!" Ningiyuk told him through her tears.

"No, child. You must give the decision much thought. Think wisely, for the rest of your life is ahead of you. I'll leave you alone to think it over. No one must disturb you." With his head still inside the doorway, he added, "Ask the Great Spirit to help you decide."

Ningiyuk sat alone with her thoughts. The things her

father said were true. She had been restless and dreamed dreams of western tribes, where life was easier. She had longed to know her own parents and to be with her beautiful mother. There had been bitterness in her heart.

But everything changed in a flash, since she knew the truth. "All I want in the whole world is my—my—Oh, no! I'm so foolish and mixed up. I must ask the Great Spirit for help. And this she did.

"Hello, Great Spirit. Thank you for giving me two fathers. They both must love me. The one I don't know would pay many foxes to get me. The one I know, and love, would lose his arm to a bear to keep me. Help me to choose wisely, for I'm so young and foolish." Her prayer stopped as thoughts of home crowded into her mind.

Grandmother Itow would be sitting outside the tent scraping skins. No one in the world knew the secrets they shared. The last one was their walk to the river at sundown. Between them they had carried Itow's pouch of mysterious spirit chasers. With a great heave they had thrown them into the roaring waters and waved them into the sea. Itow always loved the sunsets but never as much as when Ningiyuk was watching them with her.

And Kiyuk would be awakening from his sleep. How he was growing from day to day. Surely he would be missing her—at least a little bit.

Okio and Komoyiok would be on the ship together. No words would be passed between them, but they would have similar thoughts about the girl in their igloo. Somehow they were so much a part of her life that she couldn't bear the thought of living without them.

But, strange to say, the deepest yearning in her heart was for Atuk. "For she's my mother, my only mother,"

Ningiyuk knew this deep in her heart and her body shook with quiet sobbing.

The she remembered she hadn't finished her prayer to the Great Spirit.

"Thank you, Great Spirit, for being with me always and for helping me." Ningiyuk realized she had forgotten to kneel. Quickly, she was on her knees, with her chubby hands clasped tightly. "I'd like to remember the fine words the missionary uses when he prays, but I can't. I hope you understand me. I understand You. Thank You, Great Spirit, for everything."

When she raised her head, calm and peaceful thoughts filled her mind. A happy smile spread over her face; and she felt warm, right down to her toes. All the tomorrows looked rosy pink, like the sunset on the snows.

"Tell me, child, what have you chosen?" Her father appeared in the cabin doorway.

"I have chosen my igloo world!"

Komoyiok wiped the perspiration from his forehead with the back of his hand. "We leave for home in the morning," was all he said.

"Good!" Ningiyuk clapped her hands. "But I wish we were leaving right now!" Then a thought entered her head. She pulled Komoyiok around until he faced her. "Tell me, Father, how many foxes would you have taken if my other father had wanted to buy me?"

Komoyiok looked startled. Then a solemn look came over him. "One fox tail! That would be my price!"

They burst into laughter. They were still laughing when Okio opened the cabin door.

Glossary

Artigue. The Eskimo's main fur garment, similar to a jacket with a hood.

Bannock. A bread made of oat or barley flour, baked in flat loaves.

Caribou. A type of deer with broad, flat antlers, related to the reindeer.

Char. A medium-sized fish, the Arctic salmon.

Husky. A strong medium-sized dog with a bushy coat and curled tail, used as a sled dog by the Eskimo.

Hudson Bay Company. The main trading company of the Canadian Arctic, in some places the only trading post for many miles around.

Lemming. A small, tan, furry animal, similar to a guinea pig.

Ooloo. A rounded knife used by Eskimo women to scrape animal skins.

Pok-sac. A pouch made of sealskin, used as a container for seal oil.

Ptarmigan. A medium-sized, plump bird with reddish brown feathers and completely feathered feet.

Royal Canadian Mounted Police. The Canadian federal police, responsible for all policing in the Arctic region. Before modern transportation, all their arctic winter travel was by dog sled.

Sinew. A narrow, strong strip of animal tissue used as thread.

Snow platform. The Eskimo's living room. It is a shelf of snow a few feet higher than the floor of the igloo, covered with furs. This is where the family sits, eats, sleeps, and plays games.

Tomcod. A small speckled fish, similar to the codfish.

Tundra. The wide, flat, treeless plains of the Arctic region.

Umiakpuk. Eskimo word for a big ship.

DATE DUE